Devil's Ivy

C A Martin

Edited by readabit: Copy Editing and Proofreading Services Est 2018

The Lord of Lust Publications
1st Ed.
ISBN: 978-1-83502-016-6

Formatted and distributed via The Lord of Lust Publications
Cover Art by L.M. Mountford

DEVIL'S IVY

THE SAGE SAGA
BOOK ONE

C.A. MARTIN

Cash out. Pack up. Run.
Small blessings. Disguised or not, these things
come to us even if we don't think we need them.
She was looking at him so hard.
Hard enough to stop her tears from betraying
the indifference she was trying to convince him
she felt.
"Where is this coming from? Why now?" she
asked.
Silence.
"What do you want me to do?"
"Stay," he whispered.

Thank you, for showing me the door to
freedom.

PROLOGUE

British coaches are the worst mode of public transport.

Kangaroo Kid is fated to sit behind me every time I travel, pretending to be the latest trendy superhero that beats my seat into submission. My chair, always the villain of some faraway galaxy destined to suffer a monstrous defeat at the little piggies of some pre-teen. The back four rows of some outdated navy textile reek of urine and the state of the miniscule toilet is unfathomable to say the least. Other passenger's disparaging remarks had put me off using them years ago and the one time I had found myself with little choice, I had berated myself, regretting not disembarking the coach for the nearest bush. Not to mention, there is always one passenger that stows away something that smells like the dodgy curry you'd get roaring drunk at a suspicious takeaway at four o'clock in the morning. The threat to hurl my breakfast in the cesspit to my rear is indeed very real.

And there is always one girl trying not to cry.

I always used to wonder about that girl. Whenever I travelled, there would always be one, and only ever one. Blonde, brunette, short or tall. They come in a variety of beautiful shapes and sizes, and I wondered, why did they cry? An argument with a loved one maybe, or their cat had just had a one-way trip to the vets. Whatever the reason, I have always hoped it wasn't because they are sad to be alone. I had always loved to be alone, until today.

Words can't possibly describe the frustration I now have at the world and everything and everyone in it. The last twelve hours have my head reeling and my stomach in knots, twisting and turning into some kind of unrecognisable shape, occasionally fighting to overthrow the coldness lingering in my spine. I'm suffocating.

But more than anything else, the frustration at myself is making me panic and I can't concentrate on the radio's scratchy interpretation of some *Radiohead* song long enough to forget how many cities I've already passed. God knows when I'll ever learn from my mistakes. I try to remember the last time I was observing surgery in the operating room.

Cut down the linea alba.

Cut through the subcutaneous tissue.

Divide the linea alba.

Why is there always one lonely girl crying on a bus?

I remember saying to a friend once, that I couldn't understand why things would ever get bad enough for a person to actually run away. Why would someone leave their home, their work and their life behind? I loved my job. Will I still study? Can I transfer? Half way through my core training, and now it's gone.

Kangaroo Kid is at it again. I peek between the seats and make eye contact with the mud-brown eyes of some black-haired, pale tweenager. He smirks at me, his ratty little nose crinkling in malicious intent. The man I assume to be his father has a raunchy magazine pushed up to his face, oblivious to the kid's antics. I swivel back around, pushing myself deeper into the bottom of my seat, exasperated and desperate to reach my destination.

I feel motion sick.

Summer rain batters the window to my right. Trust the weather to be horrendous. It's probably some creepy foreshadowing of what my life is going to look like now. Typical, and almost laughable. Almost. I swipe away a tear that had abandoned the safety of my waterline from my freckled cheek and stare at the blur of trees as the coach continued to speed down the motorway.

This will never happen again.

I prefer my own company and don't play nice with others. I've always had my own interests and was never adopted by cliques or welcomed into the crowds. That's why I love plants. They are less complicated than people, but obviously not widely accepted as what most people would call *normal company.* Nearly everyone I've ever met has called me odd for it. Not unique, or individual. Just odd. I can never tell if it's meant endearingly. Looking back now, I think it's probably just a fact.

Another tear has betrayed its prison and assaulted the corner of my lips, trickling onto my tongue, combatting the perpetual dryness in my mouth. It tastes like salt. Salt leeches nutrition from the earth, preventing crops from growing. Historically, opposing armies would salt the other's crops in times of war to bring on famine and starvation, eventually causing one side to surrender or die. Will I whither away and die now?

I thought I could deserve love, even if I was a bit different. I am a young professional, just starting to gain a reputation for being the top of my class, and good in a crisis. Even *he* had convinced me I was valuable. If I had been as acute in understanding my own foolishness as I had in my studies though, I might have realised it wasn't love, but someone's idea of a joke.

The blur of greens and ambers continue to stroke my peripheral vision, and now I can feel the cold coming in a little closer. The dismal heating of the trans-national coach is not immune to the autumnal weather.

Is that lady's snack making me hungry or feel nauseous?

My nose is leaking, as if it couldn't get any worse. I rub my face into the sleeve of my hoodie and pull my knees up to my chest. I'm going to end up dehydrating at this rate.

I've never really liked people, despite training after medical school in placements all over the country to become a surgeon. Then again, people have never really liked me. I collect plants, have peculiar dreams, and have always been a realist, a lateral thinker. Attachment is a complex thought. My bed-side mannerisms are fully scripted and routinely practised. I was going to make the perfect surgeon, before I had abandoned my placement without so much as a letter of notice. As it would happen, I had fallen in love with someone who thought it would be advantageous to their career to crumble my self esteem, leave my confidence in ruins at the bottom of the hospital's main staircase, and desert me in the echoes of their laughter.

"You should've known Fleur, it was never real. You're such a fool for thinking someone like me could love someone like you."

The tears are flowing freely down my face now, and my lungs are begging me to let in more air so my body can sob as my heart breaks a little more.

I don't want to be that girl on the bus.

CHAPTER ONE

Alone Again

I had been lying in scratchy old quilts for hours. Geometric shapes in all colours and sizes were draped over my aching limbs, stiff from being in storage under the cot bed that had been maliciously poking each of my ribs through the thin mattress harder with each passing hour. The scent of the lilac hydrangea on the bedside was my only comfort.

The sound of the tap dripping in the downstairs bathroom was really starting to fray my last nerve. I rubbed at the dryness in my sleep-deprived eyes and proceeded to jab my left eyeball with a clumsy digit. I hissed and held my palm to my socket until the weeping slowed. It would appear my last brain cell had deserted me too.

There was snoring in the room next door containing the two people that have never let me down and another one of their waif and strays. My parents had decided in their retirement that they would run a sort of nursing home for the elderly. Sick, mangy, dogs left at the local shelters that no one else wanted had brought them a newfound joy in the absence of children in the house. One by one, my parents would take them in, medicate and care for them, and love them whole-heartedly until they passed, bone in chops and cushion under foot. They'd turned into local philanthropists, really.

Whoever was snoring sounded like a drunk trucker.

Is it one of my parents or the decrepit dog?

I loved that dog, so it couldn't be her.

Must be Mum.

Despite this house's familiar occupants, it still felt empty and strange. I'd left my childhood home at the age of eighteen and gleefully skipped straight into university housing. The rooms had been redecorated, old furniture that had been teethed on by yours truly had been replaced and any belongings I had left behind had gone into storage. But don't bite the hand that feeds you. Coming home was probably the best and worst thing that's ever happened to me.

I'd been here at least a week and I was losing track of time. They say that time heals, but how much time does it take? A week for an abrasion, maybe a month for a laceration. What about an exploded organ? A shattered reality could take a lifetime.

Time is what scares me sometimes. It slips away without notice and before you know it, you've missed some of the key moments of your own life. My eyes grew heavy as I pondered how on earth I let my young adult life slip away.

I lie bruised and bloodied on cracked cement, a wave of heat emanating from my body. I feel the coolness of the rain, but I'm still so hot. The ground is icy, frost creeping from underneath me, but steam rises from around my limbs.

I can't breathe.

Flashes of a shadow.

Burning in my finger tips.

A sadness in my heart.

Tentacles of pain reach from within to consume me, but a hand forms from the vapour in front of my heavy eyes.

I'm desperate to keep them open.

"Come to me," a soothing voice tempts.

I reach out to the shadow, accepting of any relief from the torture I feel.

My eyes begin to shutter, like the ending of an old film, and my vision blurs.

The hand disperses and a man comes to kneel above me, his arm outstretched and on his bicep, a tattoo of some bird I couldn't quite make out through the fog. Amber eyes bring my vision back to life.

"I'm here," he says.

I woke up in a cold sweat.

"For fuck's sake," I whispered, my breathing ragged and my heart thunderous. My head throbbed as I rubbed my temples, a vain attempt to push the nightmare back down to the depths of my subconscious. I'd say I was an insomniac, but I had never had trouble getting to sleep. Studying so hard for so long had taught me to sleep where I could, when I could. The minute my head touched down, I was usually a goner. Staying asleep was the hard part. The same terror would come most nights, sometimes only slightly different than the previous one.

If I wasn't dying on the floor somewhere, I was opening an ominous door or running for my life. But it was always the same. I felt like I was on fire, but cold, and it always felt like what I'd imagine death to be. They have always felt more like memories from someone else's life. Like creepers on a house's stoney walls. Weeds. Invaders.

I returned to drowning in scratchy, pokey self-pity.

Drip. Drip.

I loved my family- they loved me. They have always known that I'm not ordinary, they just don't ever say anything. It's not like I knew who I got it from either. My biological parents had never been around. Dad had always said that the day he and his wife were asked to take on a newborn ward was the best thing that had ever happened to them. They were blessed, he said, and have loved me like I'm theirs.

Unlike *he* did. I reminisced to the time I convinced myself he had genuinely cared for me.

"You do realise I'm plagued by bad luck?" I laughed.

He tucked a stray piece of auburn hair around my ear. "I think it's cute," he replied. "My good luck will counter yours and it'll be fine."

We had stayed up until dawn, laughing and joking about some of my more embarrassing moments, and what would later become his ammunition to gun down my ego. Like the time I pranced across our kitchen, trying to weave a maze in what I thought was smoke drifting up from the flat below, to get to the door and warn the neighbours of the fire. He thought it was hilarious and caught the whole thing on his phone, assuring me that there was no fire, and that I was hallucinating.

The interns had also found it funny. I still couldn't shake the sounds of their whispers as I strode through the staff lockers to throw our flat keys on the bench beside him as he hung his designer stethoscope around his know-it-all neck.

I led in my parent's guest bed, dazed and angry at myself for letting the memories flood back in. I smoothed the creases from my forehead, careful to avoid my tender left eye.

Drip. Drip.

The clock read 23:46.

We'd never actually said that we'd loved each other. After three years of sharing space, food, and holding hands in public, I had just always assumed it. I was training for my surgical licence, so was he. I was determined to make something of myself, having started my life without even so much as a last name, and he was to join a long line of gifted doctors, born to a legacy. Before we had been together, we had competed to get to the top of the class we had shared. I was the underdog, a nobody who had received grants and public funding for good grades. His way was paid by his esteemed father, who happened to own the private hospital we had both aspired to eventually establish ourselves in.

Dad had picked me up from the coach station when I arrived. I told him not to, that I would find my own way home, but he had embraced me in a crushing hug the minute I stepped off of the coach. I was grateful really, but he hated seeing me cry, and the comfort had been overwhelming. My parents were my lifeline. Anyone else had always been a little more complicated for me, but secretly I'd wished I would grow out of it. I think that's one of the reasons why I had wanted to be a surgeon. Needed by strangers I was never required to know past the operating table.

My future was mine and made until it wasn't, and now I was alone.

I glanced at the shadow of the blooming hydrangea and its bulb poking from beneath the potting soil. I decided I must tell Mum to plant them a little deeper.

Drip. Drip.

CHAPTER TWO

Day Dreamer

"Henry and I have been looking at flats in the area, petal."

I felt my face drop as my teaspoon sluggishly poked at the teabag in my favourite egg-shaped mug. "I said I was working on it Mum. Besides, Dad is still working long days and my problems shouldn't be his."

"I know, but it's been six weeks now and we just thought you'd be more interested…" My mother's voice drifted away as my concentration lapsed.

I watched as the sugar slowly dissolved on the edge of the spoon as I lowered it into the creamy liquid, each little granule slowly becoming a part of the beverage. The September sun that shone through the breakfast room's floor-to-ceiling windows bounced off of the metallic utensil, and warmed my spot at the sandy coloured oak table.

This was now my usual morning routine. I would make a ritualistic hot beverage, and sit at the table for at least an hour and a half, nursing it until it was stone cold contemplating how I was supposed to move forward with my life. So far, two of the local hospitals had denied my applications to transfer to their programmes. They weren't even particularly well-rated hospitals, but it would seem my reputation for walking out without warning, and my *"fragile constitution as a female doctor,"* had preceded me, or so the letters of rejection had said. No one would take me onboard without hesitancy now. My career was in pieces, and likely had a lot to do with a certain someone's own influence. So I would sit here, company for the dog, Tess, in her retirement and wallow.

My parents did love me, but they had long since moved on with the next chapter of their life together. I had already left home under the pretence that I would make something of myself. They had given me the tools I needed to become self-sufficient, and I had managed to wind up back in their flowerbed, a pest in their well-deserved Eden. They meant well, but the part-time cashier job I had been handed out of pity at the closest supermarket was not going to afford me a place of my own.

I closed my eyes as I attempted to drown out my mother's rambling a little more, at ease as the smell of fresh linen pervaded the room.

Amber eyes appeared behind my eyelids, followed by a sharp pain in my temples. Scattered thoughts, feelings of confusion, and then it was gone as quickly as it came. I winced, and thankfully it went unnoticed, except for Tess who let out a disgruntled puff from her snout as I shifted my position. I leant down and tousled her ears, a silent assurance that my warm foot would continue to serve as her headrest for a little while longer.

It was getting worse. My dreams- if you can call them that- had started to worm their way into my daydreams, stealing what little calmness I had left in the waking world. I felt ready to break.

"There's a nice property just down the-"

"Mum, I get it. I'll take a look later, I promise. Besides, if the general programme at Cheltenham takes my application, I'll need to be closer to the hospital."

She frowned at me, tucking her greying brown hair behind her eyes and shoving her glasses back up to the bridge of her nose in exasperation, no doubt because I had interrupted her. She'd always been a little more stern than Dad and *manners maketh man.*

My mother's name was Avery. Her mother had named her for wisdom, but she was usually the complete opposite. Academically she surpassed, and had once been a lecturer at the local university, helping me to study through medical school. However much to the annoyance of our local community, she had never mastered the art of looking both ways before crossing the street, and to my dad's dismay, still hadn't successfully managed to record more than the last five minutes of a television programme on the box. Bless her cotton socks, she did try, but some daily living skills had eluded her. It hadn't stopped her from drilling me with lessons on etiquette though. Respect and manners came first and foremost, and although she had never been cruel, I had lived a sheltered life. Instead of playground tumbles and sneaking out, I had suffered with paper cuts from local library books and chronic back pain from late night studies. It had helped me in the end, but I still wasn't convinced that she wasn't named after a bird cage.

My name was also French. Literally, 'flower.' Just another thing you can keep in a glass house.

"I still think you were silly to give up the university hospital in Leeds..."

A slight breeze curled through the open window sending the white linen nets into a graceful dance. They cascaded away from the open windows, and barely touching its plastic white pot, knocked over the weightless orchid that I had spent weeks nursing back to health that had been sitting on the sill. It had finally bloomed several days ago, pink flowers adorning its thin stem. It had curled inwards under the weight of so many flowers- a miracle given the state it had been in when I found it. I watched it fall, its impending doom inevitable as it landed on its side with a dull thud. Tess lifted her chin slightly from the floor where she lay under my chair, but also decided it wasn't worth racing to save it. For half a second, I mourned for it, then the breeze caressed my chin like a lover, warm and welcome as my mother continued to reminisce.

"...It just seems like a waste, that's all. You had so much to gain and-"

"Would you have preferred me to stay and be unhappy?"

Avery sighed. "I know you're frustrated Fleur, but Rick is a lovely young man. I find it hard to believe that a man of his… breeding would be so unkind."

"Breeding? This isn't the nineteenth century. Besides, I don't think frustrated is the right word Mum."

She popped her now-full laundry basket on the floor by the small kitchen's backdoor and scooped the orchid off the tiles. My mother dusted the plant down, like she would brush lint off of her trousers, and I cringed at the abuse of the fragile flower. She placed it back on the sill with a *clack*, tucking the nets into the window handles to secure them.

I looked at its pale pink petals, grieving the expected loss of my new friend. An orchid wouldn't survive that kind of fall, even after my rescue from its previous brush with death. I could almost feel the dismay from the gentle flower, as it too would know it was destined to transform into nothing more than a lifeless twig, its tangle of roots unable to resurrect it once more.

Shame, so pretty.

Avery huffed as she collected her basket and dropped it onto her hip, intending to move on to the task of meticulously storing each item of clean clothing away. A task she enjoyed and one I did not envy.

"It's time to move on then, petal. It's your life, you're an adult and should be making your own choices. You can stay as long as you need, as long as you make a plan. You've already flown the nest, and you're an independent woman now. You'll be driven mad if you linger much longer. Things will get better." Mum gave me what I assumed was supposed to be a reassuring pat on my hand. She gave me a motherly peck on the cheek to boot before shuffling out of the kitchen, the old spotted Tess wagging her tail and padding behind her in arthritic pursuit.

I let my eyes close, refreshed by the unusually warm autumn air that drifted through the kitchen. The room now was empty and the silence enveloped me. I could still hear the traces of morning birdsong from the line of evergreens at the bottom of the long garden, and the rustle of drying leaves from the hedgerow that skirted the fence against the desolate greenhouse that had lain empty since I moved out. In my mind, I skipped across the pool that now lay covered, and I imagined the trees and its consciousness- for surely they must have them too- retreating into themselves, preparing for the first frost of winter. They would whisper to each other their fond farewells until spring, a low, solemn hum of hibernation.

I breathed deep, opening myself in quiet meditation, and it was like I could feel the entire garden, the slow inhale and exhale as energy was both given and taken in perpetual equilibrium. I listened to the gentle noise of the flora as the breeze moved through them, into them, and around them, and as I sank further into my reflection, the hum transformed into a low, male voice.

I'm here.
My eyes flew open.

CHAPTER THREE

Jaded

It was late. The air was unusually humid for late September, and there was virtually no breeze to offer any comfort. Even the store felt muggy, rain due any hour now. I peeked out of the shop's front windows from where I sat at the till and spotted the sun creeping behind the horizon. I had done everything I could today to forget the voice that had broken my thoughts this afternoon. They had sounded as if they were sitting right next to me at the breakfast table, but when I had looked, there had been no one there. Maybe I did have a tendency to hallucinate.

The hustle and bustle of the supermarket had died down as the evening had drawn in, leaving me with less to distract me. Kids and their after-school comics as they threw *pick n' mix* at each other had vanished. Couples young and old holding hands as they purchased ingredients for their cosy dinner for two had come and gone. Families doing their weekly shops, their toddlers drooling in their trolley seats, had abandoned the store too. They had all gone now, bar a few, as people had long since returned home from their busy lives to their creature comforts, to their normalities. I envied them.

My life had been like that too, from the outside, the humdrum of routine eating away my days. Before the hospital drama and the 'hallucinations' that had ripped my reality a new one. It seemed like a lifetime ago.

When I had turned twenty-five, almost a year ago, the dreams had started, and it had all gone downhill from there.

I am cold.

I am alone.

An old building looms above me in an abandoned courtyard, crows cawing into the twilight. There are holes in the walls where the brick and mortar has crumbled away. Stained-glass windows that had once depicted some ancient story were now shattered, their fable lost in the sharp remnants on the wet ground.

The only part of the building that has been untouched by time, weather or man, is the doorway. Two dark pine doors with ornate brass handles are inset into a stone archway that is being slowly strangled by the decaying vines of a honeysuckle.

A flowerless rose bush sits on either side of the cracked steps leading up to the doorway, its menacing thorns aching to inflict pain on any trespassers.

As I begin my journey up the steps, I feel myself begin to tremble, fear of the unknown ravaging me from the inside. Every hair on my body stands on end.

I reach out for the handles to open the doors but they begin to quake, creaking and splintering, cracks radiating from its hinges.

Violet fire passes between the wreckage and the palm of my hand, the rain hissing as it touches my skin, and I flinch, drawing my hand away.

Pain.

A young woman, dressed in business attire with perfect mid-length ebony curls and pristinely manicured nails placed a bottle of Merlot, a microwave carbonara and a small succulent on my conveyor belt, breaking me from thoughts of last night's dream. I clicked the button to whir the conveyor into motion, sluggishly carrying the items towards me.

"Good evening, do you need any bags?" I asked monotonously, my mantra for the day having replaced any semblance of politeness.

"No, thank you," the woman huffed in reply, nails clacking on her phone screen as she neglected to look up.

I scanned what was most likely her dinner and dessert with two obnoxious beeps and rolled them down to the bagging area. I picked up the succulent in its tacky brown pot and yelped, as I dropped it back onto the conveyor, grasping my tingling fingers.

I stared at the young jade plant, bewildered. I eyed it suspiciously, waiting for a bee, or a spider or some other angry insect to crawl out of its hiding spot, perturbed at having its home jostled about, but none came. The common house plant had none of its pink or white flowers yet, but within seconds, its fleshy, oval shaped leaves looked greener.

Warmth rushed to my fingertips, and it almost felt like the heat of my body was flowing away, ebbing through the ends of my digits.

What on earth-

The woman cleared her throat and my head snapped up, adrenaline surging through my rigid form.

Her eyebrows were arched in annoyance, and impatience emanated from her tapping stiletto.

"I'm so sorry- static shock," I smiled, crimson embarrassment rushing to my cheeks. I scanned the barcode on the pot and carefully stood it back up, sliding it gently down to join its fellow purchases.

"That'll be fourteen-"

The woman tapped her card on the machine, scooped up her items and was gone without a backward glance, the click of her red-bottomed heels fading into the distance. I removed her receipt from the roll and placed it into the bin next to my swivel chair.

The further away she got, the cooler my fingers became, until only a dullness remained. I rubbed my hands together, contemplating the strange interaction with the jade plant.

I felt a familiar hand on my shoulder- Jess from the till next to me. Her blonde ponytail tickled her shoulders, and green eyes surrounded by heavy mascara looked down at me where I sat, her lips, full of artificial filler, pulled into a concerned pout. She pointed at the clock, our ritual for this time of day, and I nodded in silent acknowledgement.

"Are you okay?" she asked, likely having just witnessed my fumble with my last customer of the day.

I looked down, reluctant to answer. Jess knew nothing of my past and I was happy to keep it that way. The staff at the store didn't need to know me, so I diverted. "I'm just not cut out for this Jess. I'm supposed to be doing something bigger than this, I know it."

Jess squeezed my shoulder, deciding not to press me. "Have you heard back from the hospital yet?

I grimaced. Another failed application. My expression was enough for her to understand.

"Maybe you need to find a new adventure Fleur, something to really sink your teeth into. You shouldn't end up stuck here like the rest of us." She slung her jacket over her shoulder and strode away towards the back of the store to the staff room.

Likewise, I grabbed my jacket from the back of my chair and stood up, stretching as I did so after being sat down swiping barcodes for the last several hours. I collected my water tumbler and my mobile phone that I had stowed away under the counter and made straight for the clocking machine to end my shift. I would avoid the staff room just in case. As I exited through the supermarket's automatic doors, my phone buzzed.

The ID came up as Cam.

"Hello?"

"Hey Fleur!" Cam's shrill, perky voice emanated from the phone, causing my left eardrum to ring. I scrunched up my nose, knowing full well what was coming next.

"We're going out. Lane and I. You've been avoiding me for weeks and I need a drink. We're coming to get you!"

"Okay, but-"

And with that Cam had already put down the phone.

For the last few weeks, the only reprieve I'd had from my permanent, pathetic doldrums, was Cam. She was my oasis. Her new chap though, I could well do without.

We had been friends at school, but I couldn't have explained what had drawn us together. Cam, with the privilege of a right-winged parliamentary father, would sneak out, kiss boys in cleaning cupboards, and argue with teachers. I had been the complete opposite. She'd often compare me to a moose as teenagers- clunky and awkward, but determined to eat my greens and keep my nose clean. We'd barely spoken two words to each other before our ninth year, until a teacher had mistakenly called me stupid for pointing out an error in his own equation, and Cam had laid his lack of capability out for the whole school to see-including his boxer-briefs on the flag post outside. She had narrowly escaped expulsion, and we had become inseparable from that day on. We had only agreed to part ways when it was time for me to go to university and start my medical degree.

Cam had opted to backpack around the world, financed by her Westminster heritage, avoiding further education at all costs, much to her parents' dismay. Only coincidence had brought us back home again. Her parents had convinced her new self-love, peacekeeping, Bali-brain it was time to do something with her life and she had decided to become a teacher herself, taking on an apprenticeship at the local college. Determined now to fund her own choices, instead of accepting support from a father she did not politically align with, she had taken on temporary reception work at a car dealership.

That's how she had met Lane, a young, lanky salesman that oozed sleaze, but made enough to drive her around in a flash silver Skyline and tell her she was special. To her, he was the easiest way to the high life she wouldn't be able to afford without her dad.

If I didn't go home, Cam would send out a search party and I'd have no choice either way than to spend time with her and her greasy boyfriend, who was the real reason I'd been neglecting Cam. I couldn't stand the bloke, and he rarely let her out of his sight whenever they were together.

"No point avoiding it now," I said aloud, marching myself across the now-empty dual carriageway and towards my parent's neighbourhood, feeling geared up to lose my troubles to tequila and the compliments of a barman that quite frankly, probably didn't care.

CHAPTER FOUR

Swanning it

The club stank of vomit and stale alcohol but I wasn't about to let that ruin what could potentially be the stress relief I had been looking for.

At least it didn't smell like clean laundry.

I could feel the burden I was causing my parents, but with the bass rumbling the mildew-ridden floorboards underneath my favourite pair of kitten-heeled, knee-high boots, I desperately tried to let go of my guilt. I'd stumbled and fallen, I knew that, but I wasn't destined for a menial life. Change would come, I could feel it. My adrenaline levels were still high from my interaction with the jade plant, and although I couldn't place it, it felt like something in me had almost evolved into a calm acceptance of the unknown.

The Jericho Lounge was a dive, really, but the locals found it entertaining enough and it would be open later than the others, welcoming the last of the night-life connoisseurs. Located in the heart of the town centre, it was where people from all walks of life would end up. Inside, two bars graced each side of the wide entrance which was dotted with potted ferns and decorated with old movie posters. The large dancefloor barricaded by high-rise tables with no seating for anything other than the dancer's forgotten beverages was flooded with sweaty bodies, lost in their drunken haze. The only seating available in the entire club was secluded to the right of the dancefloor, where young men and women, barely into their adulthood, screamed and laughed over the prosecco they were sloshing over each other.

Off to the left of the dancefloor was the entrance to the smoking area, where Cam had been darting in and out of for most of the evening, an ever changing rainbow of alcopops in hand. At least she had been until about twenty minutes ago when she had disappeared with some tall, tailored, model-like man that definitely wasn't Lane, and I had assumed she would find her own way home, as per usual.

Cam could take care of herself, as she always had, I just wished she wasn't so frivolous sometimes. No doubt Lane would catch up with her eventually and apologise profusely for whatever he had done to entice her to leave with another man. A drunken grope of another girl, perhaps. If it wasn't for the fact that he was an obnoxious, self-centred twerp, I might have actually felt bad for him. He was painfully obsessed with her, and whatever he had done probably didn't warrant Cam's lack of fidelity.

Her mother had passed away when we were both little and her dad hadn't been around much due to his required presence in Westminster. Despite the luxuries she had grown up with, Cam would wait for the cards with his handwriting in every day for weeks before her birthday or Christmas until she was fourteen. When the cards started to come written by his secretary, she stopped caring.

I sighed, and removed my phone from the top of my boot and clicked it to life. The screen read 23:46. I cocked my head at the familiar numbers, but dismissed it within a second. It was early, but I wouldn't stay in the club alone much longer. Cam had deserted me, and as much as I was enjoying the drum and bass, I wouldn't be grinding myself up on some stranger just so they could laugh at me later. I'd rather catch fire.

I raised my empty glass to the barman to signal another drink. Within a few minutes, my third tequila on the rocks was in my hand and raised to my lips, a pesticide to my internal organs but a blanket to dull my senses a little more.

The DJ had switched from an upbeat remix to a more primal kind of mix, the bass increasing to quake the entire club. I watched the dancers, swaying and bouncing slightly with the sultry swing of heavy intoxication as the celestial feel of the song gripped them.

I swirled the ice around the bottom of my glass, appreciating the gentle *chink* as the cubes collided. I felt myself start to bob my head with the beat of the music, but was far from being drunk enough to let it engulf me completely.

My phone lit up on the bar drawing my attention back as it signalled my pre-set alarm. Midnight. The last few drops of Patrón warmed my chest as I took it straight back, abandoning the empty glass on the dark wood bar top and safely returned my phone to my boot.

"Happy Birthday Fleur," I mumbled.

I straightened the cuffs of my cream silk Ted Baker blouse, my gift to myself. It was a miracle it had remained clean. Just as I turned away from the bar to leave for the cloakroom to retrieve my bag from the bleach-blond trainee behind the desk, movement caught the corner of my eye from the other side of the more crowded bar.

I glimpsed a black-inked swan tattoo attached to a well-toned bicep, poking out of a well-fitted black t-shirt. I stopped to notice the man behind the tattoo, a sense of déjà vu crawling in the back of my brain. My breath hitched as the connection hit me.

A mass of well-kempt chestnut hair on an olive face angled in my direction. His chiselled features suggested he was probably in his late twenties or early thirties and he was the physical manifestation of health and strength- a solid, toned body, evidenced by his choice of attire. I felt my core tighten. He was the most attractive man I'd ever seen.

As if on cue, as soon as his piercing hazel eyes met mine, he began to move towards me from across the bar, gliding past the drunken crowd. Unsure whether to stay or go, I stood glued to the spot, desperately trying to remember how to flirt, throwing away my previous reservations and accepting of any attention to soothe my battered ego. Besides, it was my birthday.

In an instant, he was towering above me, inches away from me and staring me down, as if challenging me to speak first. I could feel the heat of his body on mine and my knees felt less reliable than they had moments ago.

"--N--Nice tattoo."

Damn it.

I cursed myself for being as smooth as ever.

"I'm Fleur," I offered, attempting to batter down my nerves. I wasn't looking for a rebound, but this man was gorgeous.

His eyes sparkled with amusement like I had said something funny. "I know who you are."

I batted my eyelashes in false bravado. "You do?" I queried. Cam must've already met him and pointed me out as her wingman. She'd probably clocked him as potential prey earlier in the night as she was flitting between the different areas of the club. I desperately hoped he wasn't leftovers.

He interrupted my thoughts. "We need to talk."

"We are talking," I replied, "Besides, we've only just met."

His facial features hardened. "Privately, now," he grumbled, barely audible over the music that was still pounding from the speakers.

"I-"

He'd taken me by the elbow and was rushing us towards the exit. Faculties almost intact, I halted, stopping us both in our tracks but nearly tripping over my heeled boots in the process. He might have been deadly handsome, but I was not going to be pushed around by another schmuck. I would be better than that this time.

"Woah, hold on there bud," I shouted over the chaos of a group of girls squabbling over cloakroom tickets, trying to rescue my own from my jean's back pocket. "What's the deal? You come over to someone you've never met and start ordering them around? At least buy a girl a drink first."

I tried to step away from him slightly, but he stepped with me unwilling to let go. Annoyance taking over, I brushed his fingers off of the crook of my elbow where he still gripped me, preventing me from checking my other jean pocket.

A purple flame sparked briefly as our skin made contact. Pain erupted in my fingertips and all of the air escaped my lungs, like I'd been slammed to the ground. I felt like I was on fire, yet freezing cold, goosebumps rippling across my skin from head to toe. I lurched over, trying to draw a breath but it would not come.

A door.
Running.
Dying.

Hazel eyes etched with momentary concern bore into mine. The man hissed, then swallowed and rubbed his fingers where mine had touched his.

"Ah, that really fucking hurt," he grumbled.

I couldn't breathe without feeling sick. My vision was clouded by flashing images, a play-by-play of what I've dreamed of for the last twelve months. "What have you done to me?" I demanded, sounding a little more distressed than I meant to. My eyes widened. "Did you roofie me?"

"Don't be ridiculous, of course I didn't. I'll explain everything, just not here," he urged, with an anxiety in his voice that wasn't there before. His eyes started to flick around the room.

"You can fuck right off," I retorted, resolved not to go anywhere with the incredibly handsome stranger that had just brought my terrors into my waking world.

"Please," he begged. "Someone will have sensed that, we need to go." Cool guy had started to twitch. "Someone else is looking for you, and trust me, I'm your better option." He grabbed my elbow once more and hitched me into a more upright position.

My vision spun, hurling me around the room as I lost touch with any feeling of time or place. I doubled over and puked, directly onto his black brogues.

"Beautiful," he grimaced, staring down at his designer shoes. "Okay, it's time to go now." I felt him scoop me up and my vision flickered, delirious as my body went numb.

"Hey man, is she alright?" asked a stranger's voice.

"Yeah, my girl's just had too much to drink, ya know? Got a call to come and pick her up."

Running.
"Come to me," it whispers. "I will keep you safe."
Endlessly running.

Far away, a car beeped as it unlocked. The door clicked as it opened and I was placed down on cool leather seats.

My feet hurt more with every pound on the pavement.
I have to keep running.
My lungs burn.

"Hey! Don't forget her bag!" A high-pitched, female voice shouted from my left, muffled through the window of the door that was promptly shut.

Why am I running?
Heat radiates from my skin.
Smoky tendrils curl around my legs.
I skid to stop and turn to confront my chaser.
I collide into two brown doors with ornate brass handles.

CHAPTER FIVE

Kit

I woke up in a bed that most certainly wasn't mine, drenched in sweat from another nightmare. My head pounded, like I'd been in an MMA fight and lost, and my limbs ached. I could still feel an unusual soreness in my hands, but I fingered the cotton sheets anyway, momentarily enjoying their luxurious blended texture. They were nothing like the old, well-worn quilts I'd become more used to.

I blinked my eyes open, cautious of the late afternoon sun shining through the gap in the deep grey black-out curtains as I ascertained my surroundings, anxiety gnawing at my empty stomach as I wondered where I was, and whose bed I now lay in. I was also thankfully alone.

The loft was large, with freshly polished hay-coloured floorboards and light grey walls. The furniture was modern, yet minimalist and immaculately clean. All that the spacious area contained was the large, king-sized bed that I lay in with a soft, white, faux-leather headboard, and a matching bedside table with only a lamp seated on its top. I peered across the room and over the ottoman at the end of the bed and could see a whole wall to my right lined with floor to ceiling mirrors behind which I assumed to be some kind of wardrobe or storage, and the steps that led down to an open-plan apartment, the front door located on the far side. I took careful note of it in case I needed an escape route.

I had drunk far less than what I would consider my normal tolerance for alcohol last night, and was mystified as to my current condition. I had never drunk that much, even as a younger adult. The one time I'd accidentally had too much to drink, I'd been practically catatonic, and had been lucky enough to have been at my Aunt's Christmas party and able to escape- almost- to the guest room and sleep it off on my nephew's play city rug.

I remembered the man from the club carrying me out- was it his bed I was in? A thought dawned on me. I peeked under the sheets and was satisfied to see I was still dressed, minus my boots. Maybe he had told the truth about not slipping me a roofie.

"You're awake."

I just about fell out of the bed as the dark, handsome man from the club appeared from the stairs. I clutched the frame as he drew closer, preparing myself to sprint for the door.

"Who are you?" I demanded. "Where am I, and what the fuck did you do to me?"

He strode across the room in a second, and stood at the end of the bed, any hope of darting past him dead.

"Your language is awful," he laughed, a steaming cup offered in my direction. "You've been restless for hours. Bad dreams?"

I blushed, embarrassed that he'd watched me sleep. Mum had also said I swear too much now. My manners had suffered since moving away.

I gave the cup a careful side-eye, but refused to move to take it, despite my sandy throat. Instead, tall, dark and gorgeous perched on the end of the bed and placed the offered cup on the velvet ottoman at its foot, seemingly unsurprised by my hesitance. A small smile tugged at the corners of his delicious looking lips as he carefully watched me.

"I'm Kit Dean. It's nice to finally meet you."

"I beg your pardon?" I coughed. "Finally?"

Two pools of hazel flecked with brown peered back at me as he shifted to fully face me, his leg curling up underneath him. He studied me a while longer, his brow creasing slightly.

It was then that I actually noticed him. He wore grey sweats that hugged his hips and a plain white t-shirt that stretched over his muscular biceps. Several dark tattoos lined both of his arms but only a few stood out, like the ink was fresh. I caught a glimpse of the swan-shaped outline that caught my eye last night, and couldn't help but feel drawn to it.

He noticed me noticing him, an eyebrow raised. I looked away sheepishly at having been caught.

He silently offered me the stone-glazed cup again and I glanced at it, then at him before cautiously leaning forward to take it. I held it in my hands, warmth radiating through the ache in my body. What happened last night was not a hallucination, that I knew for sure. I needed answers, and maybe this new acquaintance could give them to me.

"Where am I?" I asked again.

"You really don't know anything do you?" Kit pondered.

I immediately took offence. "Excuse me, but-"

"About what you are?"

I looked him dead in his face. "You haven't answered my questions," I retorted.

Kit sighed, another quirk at the corner of his lips. Minutes of silence ebbed by as I waited for his response, caught in an undeclared staring contest. He really was gorgeous.

"You're in my flat, about a half a mile from the Jericho Lounge."

I cocked my head and looked away as we sat again in silence for a while. This was Kit, and I was in his flat and in his bed. I was off to a great start.

My drink was still hot and my fingers still ached. I grimaced as I unfurled my hands slightly and sipped. Honey and hot water. I couldn't help the involuntary mumble of approval.

"You're favourite right?" Kit broke the silence, causing me to jump a little.

"How did you know?" I asked, surprised.

"Because it's mine, too."

My eyes shot straight to his face. I clenched and unclenched my fist. My fingers felt like they'd been slammed in a door, but there were no marks or bruises to indicate any injury.

Kit took my cup from my hand and placed it on the ottoman once more. "Your hands are hurting," he said, as he rubbed his own fingers together.

"Why is that?" I asked, massaging the tension from my wrists as I remembered his own reaction at the club, and the jade at the supermarket.

"Ah- it was sort of- a- when we touched-," he flustered, trying to explain. He looked at me, his previous air of confidence wavering. "Kind of an exchange. A transfer," he blushed.

"A transference of what?" I parried, curiosity getting the better of me. I wasn't sure I wanted to know.

He continued to fidget, picking at something imaginary on his sweats.

"Spit it out," I pressured. "You've kidnapped me, you can at least answer my questions before I end up in your body bag!"

"Body bag?" Kit mimicked, alarmed. "What kind of person do you think I am?" He visibly deflated in apparent defeat. "It's what happens when two people who share the same truthes touch for the first time. Every soul has a will, or a truthe. Two souls that possess the ability to use magike and share the same truthe, share the same…" he trailed off, embarrassed.

Kit picked his drink up and took a sip, looking very uncomfortable and flushed. "…love. It means that by the laws of my covenant, we're soulmates. Look, you're a stranger to me-"

It was then that I realised what a complete and utter joke my life was, and burst out laughing. Unable to stop myself, I continued to laugh even as Kit folded his arms, clearly unimpressed by my outburst. "I'm sorry," I choked through my laughter. "But magike and soulmates? You've got to be kidding." I wiped away the tear that had crept from the corner of my eye.

"No, no I'm not," he replied stone-faced. "You're a witch, Fleur, and you're mine."

"I've had some strange things happen to me in the past but this-" My laughter died on my lips as I swallowed, remembering all of the strange things that had happened to me in the last year. The invisible fire in my flat, the jade plant, to name a few.

Kit's expression softened, understanding evident in his expression as he realised I did indeed, know nothing.

"What kind of strange things?" He asked.

I shifted, pulling my knees up to my chest in defensive comfort, unsure if I should divulge anything further. Would he laugh at me too?

"Magike is traceable if the right- or wrong people-have been looking for it. Both have been looking for you. We got away unnoticed last night but that might not happen again. Tell me everything, and I'll answer your questions, I promise."

I'd been convinced my entire life that I wasn't normal. I'd always had a feeling I was different, but this man was talking about magical powers, like something out of a story book. I took a deep breath and closed my eyes. I wasn't sure if I believed him or not. I'd always tried to keep an open mind but this was surreal. If I went along with it, he might let me go. But what if it wasn't all coincidence?

Please give my life purpose.

CHAPTER SIX

Magike

Kit had sat and listened to me talk about the bizarre occurrences in my life for well over an hour. I had given him the basic- very basic- run down of my life too. From being adopted to my bigger life choices like becoming a doctor. He nodded and asked the occasional question, like why I chose to study so far away, who I'd met along the way. I'd obviously left out the more humiliating parts.

"I- I saw a pale green smoke once in my old flat. I thought it was fire from the floor below but my… flatmate couldn't see it. Thought I was crazy and hallucinating."

Kit tapped his upper lip in thought as he pondered what I had described. "It's a haze left by Spookes. They feed on residual energy from abstraction and then sort of go poof leaving a mist behind. They're a nuisance, really."

"Spookes?" I dipped my head at the unoriginal name.

"They're a type of dark fae. Fairies, kind of but they're husks. They don't have a soul, so no proper life. That's why they need to find abstraction- abstracte magike- to feed on. The problem is, they're minions of a shadow mage."

"But he-' I stopped myself from giving away too much. "The person I was there with couldn't see them, these Spookes," I finished.

"No one will unless they have magicke too," Kit answered. "Ordinary people can't see it at all, not even traces of it unless there's a physical change to something. It's how we've been able to stay hidden."

Open mind.

"Also sounds like you were lucky. Something else is looking for you."

"Honestly, you're speaking in riddles. Abstraction? Shadow mage? It all sounds like some nerdy board game." I shook my head.

"Um…okay, let me try to explain." He started to wave his hands around as he spoke. "Magike is when energy is drawn on to create something using a spell, or a rune. Abstraction is when magike is used without a spell or rune- it's a rarer kind of magike. All magike comes from the energy of something living, like from yourself."

"What, no wands?" I cocked my head mockingly.

"No, no wands," he rubbed his temples at the bad joke. "All magike is conjured from energy- the kind that sustains living things. With or without a tried and tested spell or a rune, magike is kind of…manipulation. You can never create it, only… transform it. Move energy from one place to another, change its form or its intended state, and as its conduit, the energy for the spell usually comes from the person conjuring it. Most witches draw it from themselves and spend years honing their skills, getting stronger, finding ways to make things require less energy, but magike always comes with a price. If you draw too much-"

"You die." I'd spent years watching life slip away from patients. People full of life one day were dead the next whether it was on my table or in their hospital bed. I understood that part at least.

"Except a shadow mage. They're the worst of us. Witches that have trained and tortured themselves to break down the barriers between them and what they call the 'Realm of The Dawn.' No one has been there and come back the same person. They live on to draw energy from other living things instead of themselves. The moment they drain the energy of something else and it dies, their eyes will remain red, even when they aren't conjuring. Killing something else," Kit grimaced, "it chips away at your soul. For each death your magike causes, the universe takes back a part of you, your truthe, until there is nothing left but hate and rage. They're incredibly dangerous beings."

"And you think there's one after me?"

"Yes, I do. So does the covenant. Probably for the same reasons they sent me to find you. It's not often one of us- a witch- stumbles into the mortal realm. And why were your powers not noticed before? If you were born to a covenant, you belong there, not here."

"But my parents- this is my home," I argued.

"You'd be too dangerous here, especially with no training."

"I'm not dangerous, I took an oath- to heal. I'm a healer!"

"Why do you think Spookes were in your flat, Fleur?" Kit questioned. "You must've abstracted. Whether you meant to or not- you're magike is rare and someone dangerous is looking for it."

I held my head in my hands, bewildered. Everything he said made sense, but it didn't. If he was lying, he was good but if he wasn't... my whole life was about to change.

Kit leaned across and gently swept a stray strand of auburn hair away from my face. It felt familiar, and I momentarily welcomed it. His touch was gentle and I instantly had goosebumps creeping up my arms, his fingers warm and soft against the side of my face. I looked up, and his fingers ceased midair. He dropped them back into his lap and averted his gaze.

"Sorry," he mumbled, running his hand through his own dark hair.

"So riddle me this," I questioned, determined to look unbothered by the physical changes his touch had caused my body.

"If I was born to magicke, why have I never known before? Why now?"

"Chances are, you have, in some small ways and just haven't noticed- we didn't. Something changed around a year ago. That's when our sages started looking for you. Our covenant elders are called Sages, and usually they would teach a witch how to use magicke. They don't know where you came from either."

I nodded, following. I wasn't sure I liked the thought of being tracked, stalked for a year of my life without knowing.

Kit stood and padded over to the door, and retrieved my bag. I took it from his hand and placed it down beside me on the bed, grateful that he had recovered it last night.

"So what happens now?" This time I couldn't keep the fear from my small voice. I already knew the answer.

"Now we leave for Anatidae in the enchanted realm. We're going to The Temple of the Sages, in the heart of Signette- my covenant."

"This is crazy. You're crazy. My life is here, I'm not going on some fantasy adventure with some Adonis I just met. If I'm a witch, you're a cave troll."

Kit's eye darkened. "Adonis?"

"Fuck off," I scowled, cursing my traitorous tongue.

Kit put his hands up in mock defence. "Look, there's questions we need answers to. Why can you abstract? And who's covenant do you belong to? That's what the sages asked me to find out by meeting you, but things are a little more complicated now. You have no idea what you are, which means you're not here in the mortal realm by accident"

"I'm not dangerous!" I growled. "I've never done anything in my life on purpose let alone conjure up some woo-woo-"

"You're so argumentative!" Kit sighed, frustrated by my apparent lack of cooperation.

"You're so rude!" I returned sharply.

"You're untrained and you're being hunted. Trust me, like I said last night, I'm your better option."

A shrill version of a nineties rock song blared to life as my mobile phone screamed contact with the outside world. Kit looked startled and then chuckled, no doubt finding my love for R.E.M funny. I scrambled through my bag and hit the answer button as soon as it was in my hand.

"You'll never guess what!?"

CHAPTER SEVEN

Devil's Ivy

Cam was content, safe and sound in her parents' six-bedroomed estate about seven miles into the Cotswolds after a 'wild night,' with the guy from the club. She'd said Lane had left her alone and he'd been draped over some skinny brunette when she'd found him. I felt less sympathy for him. Hopefully she was done with him now and she could find herself a nice man that wasn't internally ugly.

She'd also covered for me when my mother had rung asking where I was- my present hadn't been touched and my usual mug still hung on the cup tree.

Twenty six years old and I still felt like a dirty stop-out.

Grown woman my ass.

Kit had left me to take my phone call and had started pacing around his studio flat below occasionally glancing up in my direction. I peered over the edge of the loft as far as I could without getting off of the bed. He'd pick up a book. He'd put it back.

Cam had assumed I'd also gone home with a stranger. I definitely wasn't prepared to tell her any different, and Kit had stopped mid-pace when she'd asked. So much for privacy.

I had stashed my phone back into my black Fiorelli bag, tempted to hurl myself through his front door and never look back. I moved off of the bed and down the steps that led into the open-plan living area below. I spotted my boots on the floor in the adjoining kitchen area and grabbed my leather that had been hung on the back of a high stool at the island and hurled it on. It was a gorgeous apartment, but it didn't look lived in. It looked like a showroom. I wiggled my toes into my boots and tied the bow at the top, making ready to move.

"What are you looking at?" I bit, harsher than I meant to.

"You're not very nice to strangers, are you," Kit preached from across the island.

"You sound like my dad," I retorted.

He grimaced. "Definitely not your dad."

"You want to see my powers, magicke boy," I lurched. "Watch me run a mile in these heels." I moved towards the door. "I'm going home."

"Why don't you try showing me something else?" Kit said, eyebrows ceiling high as he moved from around the island and blocked my way to the door.

"I said I didn't mean to use magicke. Abstraction. Whatever."

"So don't *try*. Besides, you can't be traced here, my building is protected. There's gotta be something we can try. Is there anything you can remember doing that was out of the ordinary, or something odd you couldn't explain? Maybe we can start there."

Odd. Bastard.

"Like what? I asked, resigned.

"I'm not sure. Abstraction tends to be unpredictable if you don't know what you're doing, but there's always a definitive outcome, and you've probably been doing it on and off your whole life- more so as you got older."

I mulled over the last twenty six years of my life. I clicked my heels on the hard floor as I bounced slightly in thought. There's noth-"

Damn him.

"Like a door locking because you wanted it to, or-" Kit started.

"Flowers that never die," I mumbled.

Kit moved from the other side of the island and loomed above me, incredulous. He smelled like leather and vanilla, like a candle you'd light on a cold evening to feel at home. I shrunk a little under the weight of his gaze and slowly inhaled him. I swallowed.

"What? I like plants. The older I got, the more I kept. Dad had horrible hay fever and in the end I got banished to the greenhouse so I just grew more. Everyone always said I had a green thumb because mine never died. They… over-bloomed," I stuttered.

"Show me." Kit pointed at a terracotta pot on a small side table next to his designer, slate grey, two-seater sofa.

I evicted myself from his proximity sliding underneath Kit's outstretched arm, and knelt down to the vine, like greeting a friend. I smiled. "Devil's Ivy. Nearly impossible to kill, but you only have a few leaves?" I directed at Kit. "Never home huh?"

Kit shrugged.

I traced the venation on the few remaining shards of green with my finger, appreciating its quiet existence. I stroked the stems of the vines, like I had with my own plants often enough, jealous at the serenity of its pot, safe in its own little home and completely unaware of the harsh realities of a human life. I felt sad for its struggle though. The pathetic, artificial climate in this apartment was depressing. It was barely hanging on, its desiccated soil unable to provide it any nutrients. It felt lonely.

I scrunched my eyes tight as I tried willing the flora to whir to life, to grow, I don't know, to grow legs? Anything?

Nothing.

Not that I was expecting anything.

"I told you, this is crazy, you're crazy." I stood up and turned to him. "Nothing is happening."

Kit looked like he'd seen a ghost.

What now?

"Fleur, your eyes. They're violet."

"No they're not, they're green."

Kit remained statuesque as it dawned on me that he looked scared. My face dropped and adrenaline surged through me as I took flight, the clack of my heels echoing off of the walls as I practically sprinted across the studio and up the steps into the loft to peer into the wall length mirror.

Fuck.

Purple eyes blinked back at me, transforming my face into one I didn't recognise. I felt the warmth in my fingertips and felt the familiar pull, the ivy beckoning me back to it, like the succulent had at the supermarket. I looked at my fingers and rubbed them together as my palms started to itch and tingle.

I whirled around to find Kit close behind me having followed me up the steps. I collided straight into his chiselled chest with an audible *thud*. I rebounded and we both landed in a heap on the floor.

"Ow," I groaned, rubbing my head where it had slammed into Kit's pectorals. The heat in my fingers had stopped, the tether between me and the creeper broken.

"You're telling me," Kit grumbled, rubbing his elbow as he sat up. He looked at me, concern etched in the creases on his forehead. "Your eyes are green again. Check the bloody plant."

We pulled ourselves off of the floor and I practically stumbled down the steps, rubbing the thigh that had broken my fall, and over to the vine, intimidated by what I had seen in the mirror.

The Devil's Ivy definitely wasn't dead or dying. Half a dozen emerald leaves had grown on a new stem that had worked its way above the barren soil, dew drops glistening in their veins. It was all kinds of impossible but it wasn't. The ferns on my kitchen side in my flat, the orchid that should've died, the jade plant. It had been me all along.

I turned once more on Kit and was taken aback by the astounded look on his face as he gaped between his newly revived housemate and me. I'd abstracted. I'd given my own energy to his neglected plant and it was real. Everything he'd said was the truth. My truth.

The adrenaline continued to surge as my breathing grew laboured, panic crushing my chest as I struggled to get any oxygen.

I grabbed my bag and I fled through the door without a backward glance, Kit's voice fading behind me as I ran.

CHAPTER EIGHT

Fight or Flight

I flew down the side street that hugged the high rise flats containing the only man to ever shout my name as I ran away. As I got to the end of the street I lurched over, hands on knees and finally drew air to the bottom of lungs. A couple walking past gave me a side eye but continued walking, their whispers barely discernible. I straightened myself out and with another deep breath, turned left and found myself on the road that I knew led into town.

What the actual shit.

I was a witch, and apparently not the normal kind. Kit said abstraction was rare and I could do it by accident. Even as a witch I still wasn't ordinary. I berated myself, lightly punching my thigh in a vain attempt to wake myself up.

My life was an absolute mess. I couldn't go back to my old job- I couldn't even re-enter my career and I knew I'd become a shadow of myself doing something I hated. If I was being hunted like Kit said, then I couldn't go home either. Maybe Jess was right, and I needed a new adventure. My parents couldn't wait for me to go and I had nothing else keeping me here. But this couldn't be it, surely. I shook my head as I walked.

Maybe it was time for me to be someone else, but I had no idea how to process that.

"Fleur! Fleur, stop!" I heard Kit calling from behind me.

I kept walking.

Kit wheeled around in front of me, stopping me in my tracks. "Please stop," he huffed, waving his arms. "Please just listen to me."

I stood on the pavement, baleful and resigned. "I don't have a choice, do I?"

"You're not safe. Please," he panted. "Come back with me. We can talk about all of it and then you can choose if you want. I won't force you." He reached for my hand. The fear in his eyes had been as real as mine had been when I looked in the mirror.

I had no idea what to do next. Or where to go. The adrenaline started to dissipate and my breathing was finally back under my own control.

Kit's hand softly grazed mine. My eyes closed and I let him lace his fingers with my own. He turned and began to walk back down the pavement away from town and to the high rise, tugging me next to him. He didn't let go.

"Are you scared of me?" I whispered.

Kit didn't look at me when I spoke and continued walking. "I was taken aback," he mumbled. "But only by your eyes."

Fleur, your eyes. They're violet.

"What does that mean then?"

"It happens when a witch abstracts. It's usually a tell at what kind of witch they are, like red for a shadow mage." Kit pursed his lips.

"And what kind am I?"

He paused. "I don't know."

We glided up the steps and through the door into his studio flat, fingers still laced. Kit rounded on me then and gently removed my bag and leather jacket from my shoulders, placing them on the stand that stood proud and devoid of any other articles. He used my shoulders to walk me back to the island in the kitchen. The cool countertops numbed my forearms as I sunk into one of the stools.

Kit had flicked the kettle on and was busy preparing two more drinks with his back to me. He hadn't looked at me once.

So he was scared of me.

My gaze wandered over to the terracotta pot and I felt drawn to it, like it was a new friend that needed my company. I imagined it saying thank you, curling around my fingers in gratitude.

"So what kind of witch are you?"

My question was met with silence, and I suddenly felt the awkwardness. Kit placed another hot drink in front of me and I accepted the cup in a haze, embarrassed at my behaviour. He'd only tried to help me- to protect me. I took a sip of the beverage without thinking.

"Shit- that's hot," I hissed, feeling the burn on the roof of my mouth. I pressed my tongue to my palette to ease the sting and place the cup down as I grimaced.

Kit cocked his head slightly. "Here," he offered. He reached over and held his hand above my drink, steam coiling up gracefully to meet his palm as he drew a quiet breath. Then his eyes glowed, just as mine had done.

But they were an exotic shade of amber.

My dreams raced in the back of my head, and I froze, unable to take my eyes away from his handsome features, transformed by his abstraction as the steam ceased driving upwards, my drink visibly cooler.

I'm here.

"Who are you?" I choked. Kit reflected the same knowing expression I must've shown on my own features.

"I wasn't going to say anything until I knew for sure but I guess your eyes sort of did that for me," he started. I continued to stare, so he continued, defeated. "I had dreams too. They started about a year ago."

"What a coincidence," I mumbled, waving him on.

"About a year ago I started having dreams about a girl. Well, you, to be precise. I didn't know it was you until I saw your eyes. But they didn't feel like they were mine. It was like looking through a window. You were..." he trailed off, drawing circles on the counter with his fingers.

"Dying."

He looked away, unsurprised by my affirmation. "If you're having visions and we're supposed to be soulmates then it might explain why I've been seeing them too. The sages-"

"Will explain everything, yeah yeah. I get it," I interrupted. "I've got questions too. I need to know, so I'll go with you, but let's get one thing clear. I don't know you enough to trust you, and 'soulmates' or not, I'm not interested."

Kit's face turned expressionless.

I rubbed the cramp that had started to take hold in my neck. Soulmates. I'll be damned if I put myself at the mercy of another man ever again. My head was spinning and I suddenly felt the extremes of the day weigh on me. I looked outside and the sun was starting to set.

Miserable cow.

Kit came around the isle to where I was sitting and gently offered me his hand.

"Come with me."

CHAPTER NINE

Peared

Five flights of stairs led up from Kit's flat to a red metal fire door, a rusted chain and a sign barring further entry draped across it. Kit shuffled towards the makeshift barrier, urging me to follow as he removed a key from his pocket and unlocked the door, ignoring the 'no entry' sign.

I followed through the fire escape that led onto the rooftop only to be greeted by the warm fragrance of flowers in bloom. Flowers of every shade and size spanned the entirety of the summit of the high rise. I had walked into what felt like a modern hot house. I looked up to see an ornamental glass pavilion curved down to meet each side of the rooftop. The sun sat low on the horizon, the sky a collage of warm oranges and pinks. The air was warm having soaked up the sun and it felt more like the summer evenings that had not long faded away.

"Kit, what is this place?" I breathed. "Is it yours?" This was heaven.

"This is my escape when I come to this realm. I spend more time here than I do downstairs. That's why it's empty. I thought you'd like to see it. You said you kept plants?" He stretched his arms wide, gesturing to the surrounding greenery.

"Nothing like this," awe contorting my reply to nothing but a whisper. "But your plant inside?"

"Rescued from next door early this morning."

I shuffled down a stone pathway gently caressing the flowers as I stepped, disturbing them enough for their individual scents to tickle my nose. At the far end of the conservatory's deck was a small, white gazebo begging for someone to waste their days on, snaking jasmine on its perpetual journey up its wooden frame.

I crouched into the secluded structure, sweeping the trailing jasmine away, careful not to knock my head on its low arch as I sat on the bench pressed against the lattice at the back.

Kit placed himself next to me and breathed deep. I did the same, instantly comforted by the serenity of feeling like I was no longer in the city. The air was soupy, supplied by the copious amounts of oxygen the foliage was producing.

"You've used magike to create this? I asked.

"Yes, in a way. In answer to your question, I'm an elemental witch but I can only manipulate the elements. Like cooling water, or contorting the earth. I still had to plant them and spend time raising them. I can't help them grow by feeding them energy like you did."

I looked to my right.

Pyrus Communis D'Anjou.

"It's a shame this type of pear doesn't fruit until spring," Kit commented.

I fondled the leaves on the small tree and patted the soil of the pot that it stood in. I wanted Kit to have one. I left my palm face down on the soil as I breathed deeply.

Kit smiled, feeling my intention, and leaned closely over my lap to watch, placing a hand on the back of the bench. He was close enough for me to feel his body move against my back as he inhaled. He exhaled and his sigh tickled my neck, goosebumps erupting on my skin.

Warmth began to grow in my fingers as I begged the fruit tree to produce a single pear, to show me that this was who I was, and that I could succeed. I needed to prove that I could do this. That cutting people open wouldn't be the only thing I would ever be good at.

I looked back over my shoulder to amber irises flecked with shades of gold and brown, inches away from my own. They swam with a primal need I didn't recognise. My heart raced and I heard my pulse beat in my ears as I tried to calm the heat that had flooded into my abdomen. His tongue flicked out to wet his lips as his eyes darkened.

Kit placed his free hand on the base of the trunk next to mine reluctantly drawing my attention back to the task at hand. I felt the tree shift and watched as creamy white clusters of flowers blossomed on a lower branch. I was entranced by my own abilities. I felt the connection between me and the tree strengthen, and I could almost feel a sing-song voice in my head, of growth and beauty and a yearning for the creatures that would come for its pollen and reincarnate it somewhere new each year.

You must have two, it whispered. *They belong together.*

Tendrils of pale lilac energy flowed from my outstretched hand and into the damp earth. I felt the perspiration begin to form on my forehead as the tree took what it needed to grant my request.

Two firm, green pears soon replaced the bundle of blooms and I watched on, enchanted. As they began to take on a yellow tinge, Kit placed his hand on mine.

"Don't, Fleur. You've given enough of yourself away. Tell it no more."

I lifted my hand as I did just that, and my hand grew cold as the link snapped. The song in my subconscious drifted away and I suddenly felt despair at not knowing how it ended. An ache immediately took hold of my whole body, like I had spent an afternoon at the gym and I touched my fingertips to the sweat on my brow.

"It will only take as much as you give, but it will take it all if you let it," Kit patted my knee. "Here." He plucked the pears from their branch and placed one in my lonely palm, leaning back into his side of the mahogany bench, the proximity increasing between us again. "Happy birthday, by the way."

I visibly swallowed and gratefully accepted the fruit. As I held it in my hands, I thought of mum and dad, wondering where I was. The words rolled off of my tongue before I could stop them.

"What's going to happen now? I can't go home, can I?"

With a sympathetic shake of his head, Kit confirmed my prediction. "Give them a call, but don't tell them where you're going. It's the only way to keep them safe."

"These sages. They'll tell me who I am, won't they?"

He nodded.

"And what I am?"

Leaning forward so that his arms rested on his knees, he nodded again, clutching his gift.

Scared or not, I had to justify my quintessentially small life. I had lived a good childhood despite not knowing who my birth parents were. Henry and Avery had raised me since birth and had pushed me to be the best I could be, even if I had felt some need to prove I could do it on my own. I'd been safe, but not protected from the harsh words of others and so I had always kept myself distanced from other people. A sheltered childhood had caused me to grow up naive, thinking I would be accepted when I had finally ventured out on my own. I wasn't attempting to justify or defend other peoples' actions, but if I had known sooner, I might have saved myself the heartbreak.

Each day felt the same, always feeling like I was searching for something. The acceptance I craved wasn't here.

I rolled the pear around my palms, appreciating its speckled skin as I rose off of the bench and towards the rim of the pavilion, placing a hand on the cool glass. As I overlooked the city's sparkling skyline, I recalled a lifetime of memories spent living a life I should never have belonged in. I felt claustrophobic as the sun made its last bank on the horizon.

I'd grown up in a glass house after all.

"When do we leave?"

CHAPTER TEN

Fate

We'd returned down the fire escape and back into his apartment as the sun had set. He's disappeared up into the loft for some time, leaving me alone in the flat below. I picked up my phone and tapped the screen, bringing up my father's contact. I punched the green button to initiate the call. It rang twice.

"Fleur! Where have you been! Cam said you were with her but we worried when you didn't call yourself." My father's stern tone was all too familiar these days.

"Hey Dad, I'm fine, it's just been a bit of a… whirlwind of a day."

"You're a big girl now darling, but at least have the good manners to let us know if you're staying out. Your mother's not too impressed. And if you're out with a new boy-"

"Hey, I-"

"When will you be home?" Henry asked.

"That's just it Dad, I won't be for a while."

His voice on the other end of line paused. I could hear the TV in the background becoming silent, having clearly been clicked off. "Are you in trouble, sweetheart?"

"I- I don't think so Dad. But, I have to go away for a while. I'll be home soon, I just don't know when."

Another pause. "Ah, they found you."

My heart plummeted to the floor as I stared at the phone in utter disbelief. What did he know?

"Dad-"

"No darling it's alright, don't say anything, they probably told you we were being watched? Someone left the sigil of Anatidae on my windshield this morning, so you're safe if you're with them. You have to go. Leave your mother to me. Just be careful, okay? I love you."

The line went dead as he ended the call and I was left with an empty hole in my stomach. Henry knew about Anatidae? Then he knew about magike and where I came from and hadn't said anything for twenty six damn years. But Kit had said his coven didn't know why I was here. I felt my anger boil. Someone was lying to me.

"What's wrong?" Kit had returned from the loft and was rummaging through one of the top drawers in the kitchen and recovered a small chunk of worn chalk.

I resolved myself in that instant to not say anything. I had to be sure that Dad was right, and that I was safe but I wouldn't know until I could ask these stupid sages myself.

"Nothing, I'm fine." Kit spared me a glance, but decided not to push it. "So how do we get there?" I asked. Maybe this city was on some deserted island with white sandy beaches where I could lay with a cocktail in peace. "I definitely wouldn't mind a private jet, or a nice yacht," I teased.

"It's the enchanted realm. The only way to pass through is by magike," Kit gestured with his piece of chalk, clearly missing my lame attempt at humour.

Kit padded over to the centre of the living room in the wide space between the kitchen and the sofas. He crouched down and drew a large circle on the floor around himself with his sedimentary rock. Within that circle, he drew three spirals, connecting them diagonally to the outer rim. I tried to peer around him to see what he was doing. Several odd chalky squiggles I didn't recognise now sat on the outside of the diagram.

He had changed into denim jeans whilst I had been on the phone, and I couldn't help but notice how his tattoos were still visible underneath the cotton as it stretched across his hunched shape as he drew. Or how his jeans hugged his waist better than his joggers had.

He stood up appearing finished and dusted the chalk off of his hands on his jeans, leaving faint streaks down his powerful thighs. He placed the chalk down on a side table and his firm gaze met mine.

Kit crouched on the slate tiled floor once more and placed his palm flat on the bottom of the picture. He whispered something I couldn't hear and the spirals began to glow, like moonlight reflecting on a lake.

My hair suddenly stood on end, like lightning was about to strike. The atmosphere in the room shifted and the air felt charged. A sharp twinge shot through my temples like a bullet and I gripped the counter. White-knuckled, I tried to steady myself.

Two brown doors.

Bloodied feet.

"I am here."

I felt motion sick as the room spun in and out of focus. Nausea hit my stomach as vertigo took over my body.

Kit's hair also stood on end, like he was falling through the air but he hadn't moved. His figure blurred- there were two of him, then only one as the room continued to spin. As he finished mumbling, he stood up and turned to me. He must have seen the pain on my face as he rushed over to me.

"Fleur, what is it?" He gripped my shoulders. "Talk, tell me you're okay."

"I just- my head. I'm- I'm not sure. I feel dizzy and sick." I rubbed my temples, embarrassed at feeling so helpless.

He studied me, catching me out in my omission. "The visions will get worse."

"I never said-"

"You didn't have to. If there's one thing people don't do around me, its lie," he forced out. "Up on the roof, I talked about my dreams. Figured you must be having them too. Besides, you sweated through my sheets."

"They've only gotten worse since I met you," I said desperately. I was scared. I was dreaming about my own death. How could I not be? I clutched Kit's arms as the queasiness began to pass and the throbbing in my brain started to dull. His gaze softened as he pulled me closer to his chest. He rubbed small circles on my lower back and as if my body knew it was him it needed, breathing became easier once more. His embrace was unselfish, undemanding. I let my body sag and the tension in my muscles eased. I could see lights twinkling through the window as the city whirred to life. It all seemed so far away now.

"The visions- it just makes things a little more complicated. And more the reason for going."

"Why are you so fucking cryptic all the time!" I feebly shoved him away from me.

He laughed a little, his seriousness from before having been extinguished from his features as he held his hands to his chest, feigning that my weak push had hurt him and half-tripping across the living room. "I don't know enough to tell you myself. But they do." He pointed at the glowing sigil on the floor. "Are you ready?" He beckoned me over to where he was standing in the centre of his masterpiece.

"And what is that supposed to do?"

"It's a door."

"It's a what?"

"Trust me," he smiled, stepping back and offering his hand.

I hesitated, but I moved to take it, and he tugged me over to stand in the centre of the circle with him. Kit reached down, collecting my other hand, gently caressing the back of my palm.

"Nos volo…" he continued to mumble.

The air around us crackled, amber light radiating from Kit's entire frame. Smoky tendrils began an intricate dance around my ankles, emanating from the chalk drawing on the floor. The mist began to rise, encompassing our bodies as Kit continued to speak, but I couldn't hear him, the blood in my ears thrumming too loudly. I focused on Kit, panic climbing up my throat as he began to cast his spell.

He gently squeezed my hands and offered me a reassuring smile as amber light engulfed us. He nodded.

"It's okay, I'm here."

CHAPTER ELEVEN

The Avenue

I dropped to my knees on damp, cold gravel and spewed everything but my memories. Flashbacks of the last twenty-four hours battered the inside of my skull as pointed rocks bit into my shins, no doubt leaving welts in their place.

I was a witch. Kit, a tall, dark and handsome stranger from my local club, was also a witch, tasked with finding me and bringing me back to the people who could tell me where I really came from. He was the man that had made my nightmares a reality and we'd just been swallowed by a fiery hole.

I was under undue stress, really.

"Do you puke a lot?" I heard Kit laugh from behind me.

I coughed, wiping my mouth on the back of my leather's sleeve. "It's not exactly been an easy day, ya know?"

"I'm only kidding. You'll get used to moving through gate sigils, but it might take a couple of tries."

"Wonderful."

The sigil had thrown us inside a cave with high stone walls that reached far above us and provided no sunlight. At first, the cave appeared grand in the dark, like castle walls, but I could smell damp, and as I peeked through my hair, I noticed rivulets of water trickling over the moss that protruded through the cracks, ruining any facade of grandeur.

Kit bent down and patted my back like I was his mate. It was a far cry from more romantic contact we'd had moments before. I clumsily gathered myself and abruptly stood, my head swimming at his overly-friendly touch. I stumbled, not anticipating my legs to wobble. As my knees gave way, Kit hooked his arms around my waist, preventing me from crashing to the ground for a second time.

Face to face, I tried not to waft vomit-breath in his direction. His face was almost expressionless, and I could see my own reflection in his irises. The corner of his mouth raised slightly as he gently bolstered me up, my traitorous footing scrambling for purchase on the uneven terrain.

We stood like that for what felt like minutes, his arms wrapped around my waist as I clung to his hardened shoulders through his cotton shirt. He was warm, and my own warmth had started to spread throughout the rest of my body, kindling the embers at my centre that I had continuously forced dormant since I'd met him. I pushed my thoughts down as I felt my cheeks warm and sweat form under my palms.

He slowly let go, my feet now rooted to the ground. I crossed my arms, hugging myself.

"What now?"

Kit gestured his head to the right in answer and my head followed, seeing only a stone wall. "This is The Avenue. It's like a corridor, I suppose, at the very centre of Anatidae. There are three passages here, one for each coven. We will cross over to the Temple- through the passage that leads to Signette."

Not for the first time, I gave him a questioning look, unsure what he meant. I visually searched the wall's cracked surface and saw nothing that would resemble an exit- or an entrance.

"Don't worry, no one can see it. It's hidden for good reason- the door. It's bound by a protection spell. Kind of like my flat, but the sigil to pass through keeps it hidden all the time." He took my clammy hand and led me over to the wall I had landed in front of, courtesy of Kit's gate. He lifted my hand up to the wall and placed it on its slick surface. "Look closely," he instructed, as he gently guided our digits over its flaws.

I felt something unseen vibrate through my hand up to my elbow as an indistinct shape took form beneath my now less than perfect medical student's manicure. A small black circle with a triangle inside, no bigger than the rim of a teacup barely stood out from the rock and I immediately snatched my hand away, a sinking feeling threatening my quiet panic. The pull had felt familiar, and I had a horrible feeling niggle at the corners of my brain.

"What is that?" I asked, frowning at the two-dimensional squiggle that had given me serious jitters. "It doesn't feel...nice."

"That's because it's not really, but I'm surprised you noticed with no study," Kit replied as he rubbed his chin. "The spell was put there long before the three covens came and it's actually one of the reasons why our ancestors chose this place. Eternal spells aren't exactly light magike though. They take immense power to create. We still don't know who put it there. But the sigil's eternal protection does afford us some stability. Our coven's been here for over six hundred years now. It's allowed us to grow. It's probably why we don't fit the stereotype of a bunch of witches either."

"Six hundred years. That's a long time?"

"Some don't have the luxury of being hidden for long, or just don't want to be. Some covens travel a lot, or can't find somewhere safe to settle for long. Ever had your palm read at a fair?" He winked.

"Are they all witches?" I asked incredulously.

"Not all no, but some are. You've just got to know where to look," he grinned.

I smiled, trying to imagine Kit dressed up as a carnival's travelling fortune teller, complete with false moustache, crystal ball and a golden genie suit. I almost laughed out loud, but Kit's face had grown serious.

"We need to go. They'll be expecting us."

I swallowed. "This is it? Through that thing?" I pointed at the sigil.

"No," Kit shook his head. "Not through, we- never mind, I'll tell you how it works later." He laughed, his eyes lighting up. "Are you ready to meet my coven?"

This was either the coolest or the stupidest thing I'd ever do, and it's not like I had a life to go back to. It was all or nothing now.

I nodded and Kit took my hand once more, placing his right hand over the gloomy mark. The air stirred slightly and the triangle emitted a faint amber glow. "Da nobis transitum," he whispered.

The rock face shimmered in front of us, and I was no longer looking at slimy moss. Beautiful mahogany parquet flooring appeared below my feet as Kit walked me into a grand open space the size of a ballroom. The ceiling was extraordinarily high, with wide beams spanning its breadth and a large wagon-wheel style chandelier hung from above, its candles lit and flickering in the shadows above.

Rainbows trickled over my black boots as evening light streamed through stained glass that sat floor to ceiling, depicting some kind of celestial story. A black-haired woman in white stood on a rocky ledge and held an orb in her hands, shards of light splintering from it. At her feet, a man kneeled- in praise or fear I wasn't sure. A forest lay behind her, a wide waterfall interrupting the sparkling treeline that pooled into the lake below.

The familiar smell of gladioli replaced the damp, and the yellow and white sources sat in beds that elegantly lined the bottom of the walls, broken only by a small wooden door that looked shabby and out of place in the grand lobby. It had cast iron fixings that suggested it belonged in a barn or a shed- not in the halls of what I assumed to be the temple's entrance.

"Young Kit," boomed a voice, echoing off of the chamber walls.

A hooded figure cloaked in emerald velvet stood previously unnoticed in the corner to the left of the door. I was slightly taken aback, feeling fooled by the false sense of quiet I had felt. The regal man was partially shielded by the refracting light of the stained glass windows, his face cast in shadow. His robes fell to the floor, concealing all but his boot-clad toes. He held his hands together in front of his tall, bulky form, a key hanging from his grasp, no doubt for the door he guarded. "Welcome to Templum Sapientia. We have been anticipating your return."

CHAPTER ONE

Luca

The evening sun shimmered through the ostentatious stained glass windows as my heart hammered, my pulse throbbing in my right temple. Fear at what lay before me gripped me and my feet rooted to the parquet flooring beneath me.

I was a witch, inextricably linked to Kit, a gorgeous stranger who had found me in a bar on my twenty sixth birthday and now I was on some real life version of a fantasy quest to find out why I was abandoned. I was afraid.

The cloaked stranger slowly opened his arms outwards in a wide greeting to Kit. His imperial voice echoed off of the empty space. "The Elders wish to-"

"Luca," Kit grinned.

The figure deflated, his size shrinking slightly as his shoulders slumped and he pulled his hood down, exposing a bald head attached to a smiling face covered in fading tattoos. "Aw man, I was tryna be all serious like, why'd ya have ruin it?"

"She's had a rough day- right?" he nudged me and chuckled.

I stood planted to the wooden floor unsure whether to respond, my temper flaring as embarrassment churned in my chest and my fear dissipating. Not that it mattered, as I was soon forgotten at the edge of the room.

What a prick.

Kit had left my side and strode across to Luca, shaking hands with him in brotherly familiarity. "You look ridiculous! What the hell are you wearing?"

"Ah- I pulled these out of the home room's drama supplies. When I heard you had left the mortal realm, I couldn't resist," Luca chortled.

"Can't leave you alone for five minutes man." Kit took the key from Luca and deftly placed it in the brass lock on the old door. "I hope you intend to give that thing back, you haven't taken a drama class in years. What were you doing at the school anyway?"

Luca's chest puffed back up in pride. "I'll have you know, I was teaching."

I watched as Kit nearly doubled over, his laughter catching me off guard as all seriousness left his features completely for the first time since we met.

"What do you mean you were teaching?" Kit stammered through his tears. "You hated school and swore you'd never go back before we even graduated."

"You've been gone for weeks man, what else was I supposed to do? Dev's been asking me to sub for months. Besides, he didn't really give me much choice after the whole wheelbarrow thing."

Kit continued to laugh at his friend's expense, and I found myself smiling with him. Luca had all of the physical traits of someone you wouldn't want to bump into at night in an alley. He was dauntless, built like a tank, and would fit the bill of your typical mobster's bodyguard. But as soon as he spoke, he had transformed into someone gentler.

An oddity like me.

"Anyway, what gives?" Luca laughed back. "I knew they'd asked you to do something important but you should've been back weeks-" His smiling eyes landed on me from the other side of the room and his words died as he finally remembered I was standing there. "Oh."

Well, I was definitely used to that response.

I gave a small wave. "Hi, I'm Fleur."

Luca looked at me, then at Kit, as recognition dawned on his inky features. "Is that- You found her?"

Kit mumbled in affirmation.

I waved my arms at Kit. "Does everyone know about me except me?" I asked, exasperated.

"Can you not get so defensive?"

Kit waved me over to join them and I just about lost it. Twenty six years of people tip-toeing around me and my weirdness. Twenty six years of getting told I was overreacting, or not behaving the way I should. I'd be damned if another man brushed off my feelings, tal, dark and whatever or not.

I nearly ran at him, my boots clacking on the wood as I sped towards him, my hands fisted at my sides. "Defensive? I'll show you defensive!" I pointed my finger straight at him as we stood less than a foot away from each other. "Why does everyone and their Aunt fucking Sally seem to know about-"

"Oi. Pack it." His own finger had risen to point at me, his eyes flaring slightly as his temper matched mine. Kit moved his finger to point at Luca. "He's part of the small- very small- group of people who knew where I was going and what- who I was looking for. Don't get yourself all twisted up. Besides, this is a sacred hall. Mind your manners and stop swearing." His eyebrow raised to challenge me but my pointed index fell to my side as the bubbling anger in me subsided, its waves lulling like the tide going out. And I felt stupid. Kit also lowered his hand, a small flush creeping under his hazel eyes as we stared at each other, neither willing to be the first to speak.

Defensive. I thought I had every right to be defensive given the circumstances. I hadn't known him for more than a day yet Kit had shown up out of the blue, turned my life upside down and told me I was his all in the same breath. He'd ruined any chance of my living the normal life I'd craved for so long. What was normal? Maybe normal wasn't suited to me anyway. It never had been before, so had I been kidding myself this entire time? He was right. All he had done so far was try to help me and I'd overreacted. My breathing felt heavy but my heart had stopped pounding in my ears. My mirrored anger dissipated from Kit's swirling irises and our rooted bodies relaxed.

Kit cocked his head. "Are you okay?"

I nodded. "Better now."

Luca was grinning from ear to ear at our altercation. "That was intense."

Kit squeezed my shoulder and turned back towards the door. He turned the simple looking key in the lock and a faint click signalled its release. The old door creaked open to a small passageway lined with lit torches as the scent of old oil drifted through.

"Time to go," Kit said, as he laced his fingers with mine and gestured for Luca to lead the way.

We walked along the curving passage until a faint evening twilight greeted us at the other end. We emerged through the open end of the tunnel into a round cobblestone courtyard. It had just rained, as the ground was wet and the air was fresh. In the centre laid into the ground was a flat, circular grey stone and another sigil, only this one was a few metres big and surrounded by Latin phrases. Small trees circled the courtyard, broken by an ivy arch on the opposite side of the passageway we had come though, and beautifully kept gardens lay beyond. On the other side of the hedges that hugged the pristine lawns were the shapes of buildings.

We hurried under the arch and through the gardens that whispered sweet nothings and onto a street. I longed to go back and explore the flora, its quiet hum a magnet to my magike. Kit let go of my hand and I missed the security instantly but was grateful for the change of pace as we slowed down. "This is the village where our coven lives. Most of them are witches."

"Some aren't?" I asked.

"No," Luca interjected. "Some are humans, but they live with us as part of our coven. It's rare, but we're not really your typical coven of witches."

Explains why I'm here I suppose.

"Kit said something similar earlier. Why are they here?"

"Because they provide a different value. Like our economy. They have better knowledge of the mortal realm, and better access when we need to travel there. They don't get traced like we do because they don't have magicke."

Luca led us through the winding roads of the small village until we stood in front of a much larger building than the little shops and terraced houses we had passed and the first stars had since appeared in the sky. Stone pillars at the foot of the structure rose to meet a pyramid that housed a large golden clock with only hands to show the time. Ebony doors with golden rings sat shut. Tinted windows with cast iron bars over their fronts were symmetrically placed around its entirety, giving the impression of prison-like security.

Kit walked up to the door and waved his hand over its right side and an inverted s-shaped sigil appeared like the one in the cave had, emitting a faint amber light. This time though, he said nothing, and the door swung inwards.

As he turned to beckon us through, I caught a glimpse of the fading amber in his hazel eyes.

So abstracting opens this one.

I stepped inside to something that resembled a dentistry office. The nostalgic smell of antiseptic and a sterile environment replaced the scent of fresh rain as we rounded on a tiny reception desk. I recalled my interview at the hospital, regret surging through me as I wondered if I would ever hold my own scalpel again.

"We're here," Kit mumbled into my ear, the hair on the nap of my neck dancing at the attention.

A small lady, easily in her mid sixties peered up at us through half-moon spectacles chained around her neck, as she placed a phone back on its receiver. She lit up as soon as she saw Kit.

"Ah, there you are dearie," she preened. "Go on in, they're waiting."

About The Author

C A Martin is a typical coffee addict, workaholic, and blessed homemaker. She has travelled to several countries and has studied abroad, gaining degrees in Liberal Arts, Theatrical Production, Business Administration and maintains several undergraduate distinctions.

Mother to two, and gifted with a stepson, C A Martin is now settled and raising her family in the heart of Gloucestershire, England. Known for being frustratingly eloquent, she has finally published.

Also by C.A. Martin

Princes are born, but legends are written with blood and steel.
As first crowned prince of Infaria, the Empire that stands in the centre of the world, Vaan has lived in the shadow of his forbears.
A master swordsman with no one to fight but his sword master, he dreams of riding to battle as his father and grandfather had done, and proving himself worthy of their legacy, and their throne.
Yet dark things are plotting to change the shape of the map, and as Vaan prepares to enter the game of thrones, where the dangers of battle pale to those of court, war comes to set the empire ablaze.
Alone and surrounded by foes that would deny him, it will take all his strength, skill and cunning to survive as he takes his first steps along the paths of destiny.
But will his road lead him to glory or damnation?

www.ingramcontent.com/pod-product-compliance
Lightning Source LLC
Chambersburg PA
CBHW030824060726
47590CB00004B/1388